THE CROSS IN THE EGG

The Easter Story Retold for Children

Shirley Taylor

Illustrations by
Wendell E. Hall

August House Publishers, Inc.
LITTLE ROCK

10 9 8 7 6 5 4 3 2 1

LIBRARY OF CONGRESS CATALOGING-IN-PUBLICATION DATA

Taylor, Shirley Ann, 1940-
The cross in the egg / story by Shirley Ann Taylor ; pictures by Wendell E. Hall.
   p.   cm.
Summary : Having met Jesus in the Garden of Gethsemane and followed him to Jerusalem, Rabbit experiences the wonder of the Resurrection and gives away colored eggs to remind children of the gift of eternal life.
ISBN 0-87483-549-6
1. Jesus Christ--Resurrenction--Juvenile fiction.
[1. Jesus Christ--Resurrenction--Fiction.   2. Rabbits--Fiction.
3. Easter eggs--Fiction.   4. Easter--Fiction.]
I. Hall, Wendell E., ill.   II. Title.
PZ7.T21785Cr   1999
[E]--dc21   98-32229
Manufactured in Hong Kong

The paper used in this publication meets the minimum requirements of the American National Standards for Information.
Sciences-permanence of Paper for Printed Library Materials,
ANSI.48-1984

To Lee and Kerrie,
and Katy and J.P. Walt

Acknowledgments

First and foremost, I thank my Lord and Savior, Jesus Christ, for it is about His love that I have written.

My deepest thanks go to three people without whom this book would not have been shared with you: Ted Parkhurst, who saw the vision; Elizabeth Parkhurst, whose abilities are truly remarkable; and Wendell Hall, whose illustrations brought Rabbit to life and captured God's love on canvas for all to see.

My special thanks to the children of my Altheimer United Methodist Church family – Alan, Allison, Andy, Ashley, Christian, Dillon, Jess, Leah, Paschall, Ryan, and Ryland – whose love inspired *"The Cross in the Egg."*

And to my work family, thanks for sharing your faith and belief that anything is possible through Christ our Lord.

Years ago, a rabbit lived in a garden called Gethsemane. Rabbit enjoyed basking in the warm sunshine and soft breezes and playing games with Squirrel, Owl, and Mrs. Hen's baby chicks. Life was good for Rabbit and all the creatures who lived in the garden.

One warm spring day, Rabbit heard voices in the garden. Crouching low in the bushes, he saw four men walk past him. The leader, the one the other three called Jesus, said, "Sit here, while I go and pray." The three men watched Jesus walk away to be alone.

Rabbit cautiously followed Jesus. His ears stood straight as Jesus prayed: "My Father, if it is possible, let this cup pass from me; yet not what I want but what you want."

Rabbit drew closer until his fur touched Jesus' robe. As Jesus prayed, tears fell from His face. One teardrop fell onto Rabbit's head, right between his ears. Jesus slowly reached toward Rabbit and touched the place where the tear had fallen. Rabbit's heart was filled with joy and love.

After Jesus rejoined his friends, Rabbit returned to his nest. The love remained inside his heart, as well as the sadness that Jesus had felt. *I wish I could make Jesus feel better,* he thought. *Perhaps a gift would make Him happy.*

Rabbit found sweet, wild berries, brightly colored leaves and flowers, stones glittering in the brook. But nothing seemed quite right. When he stopped to rest next to Hen's house, she asked, "What's wrong, Rabbit? You look so sad."

"Oh, Mrs. Hen," he cried, "I have met Jesus! He was right here." He told her of his search for a gift for Jesus.

"I have only one egg, Rabbit," she replied, "but you are welcome to what I have. Let me speak to the other hens and see if they will give their eggs for Him." Hen soon returned, carrying a brown basket that held twelve perfect eggs.

Rabbit carefully hopped back to his garden home with his fragile treasures. "I have an idea!" he said to himself. "I'll gather blueberries, blackberries, strawberries, and sunflowers. I will make these eggs the most beautiful colors in all the world!"

Rabbit asked Owl to help him select the freshest berries and flowers in the garden. He boiled them slowly to make the right colors. After he had colored the eggs blue, purple, yellow, red, and green, Rabbit looked at the basket.

"Oh my, I don't think this plain, brown basket will do," Rabbit said to Owl. "God has filled my garden with flowers, and I will pick the best for Jesus." He carefully wove wild roses in and out and around the sides.

Rabbit filled the basket with grass, making a nest to protect the eggs. As he gently placed the eggs into the nest, one of them cracked.

"Oh, no! How could this happen?" he cried.

"Calm down, Rabbit," Owl advised. "Why are you so upset?"

"Oh! Just look at this egg! The color is the most beautiful of all, but it has a crack. I can't give Jesus an egg with a crack in it!"

Owl carefully examined the broken egg. "I wouldn't worry, Rabbit," he said. "It doesn't matter to God if we are perfect or broken, He loves us just the way we are. Jesus will love the broken egg as much as all the others."

Rabbit had never known Owl to be wrong about anything. So he gathered the basket and hopped in the direction he had last seen Jesus.

"Which way did Jesus go?" he asked Squirrel.

"He took the road to Jerusalem," Squirrel replied.

Rabbit started down the road, following Jesus.

"Rabbit, wait!" shouted Owl. "You can't go to Jerusalem. It will be very crowded. The people will run over you and step on you."

"I must follow Jesus, no matter where He leads," Rabbit answered. "I will be fine. Please don't worry."

By the time he reached Jerusalem, Rabbit was exhausted. *Maybe Owl was right,* he thought. *I have never seen so many people.* He hid behind a stand of rocks until darkness fell. The city grew deserted and silent. He searched street after street but did not find Jesus.

21

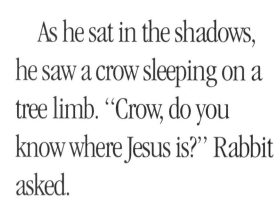

As he sat in the shadows, he saw a crow sleeping on a tree limb. "Crow, do you know where Jesus is?" Rabbit asked.

"Go home, Rabbit," Crow replied. "Jesus is dead and buried. I saw soldiers crucify Him on a cross."

Crow shivered all over down to his long, black tailfeathers.

"No, it can't be!" Rabbit cried. "You must be mistaken."

"Well, if you don't believe me," Crow screeched, "go and see for yourself! A man took Jesus and buried Him in a tomb and rolled a stone in front of it."

"Tell me how to find this tomb," pleaded Rabbit.

It was almost dawn when
Rabbit reached the tomb
where Jesus had been taken.
But something was not right.
The stone was rolled away
and the tomb was empty.

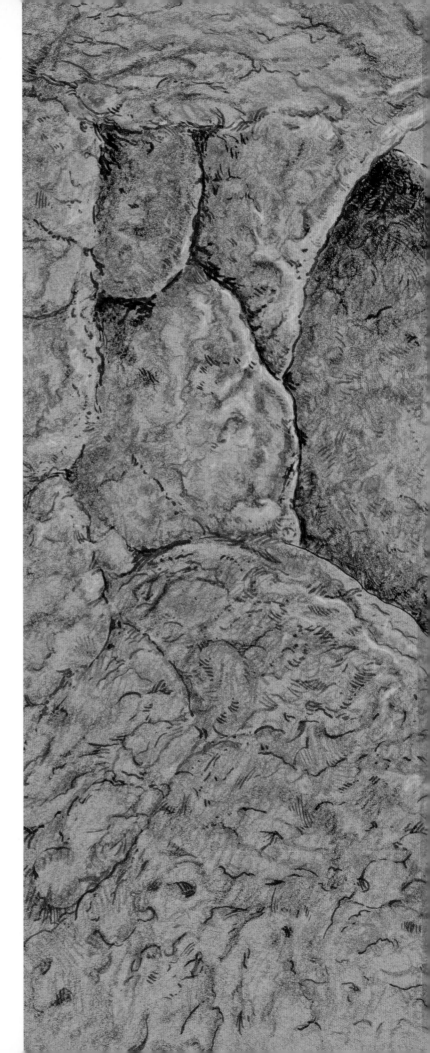

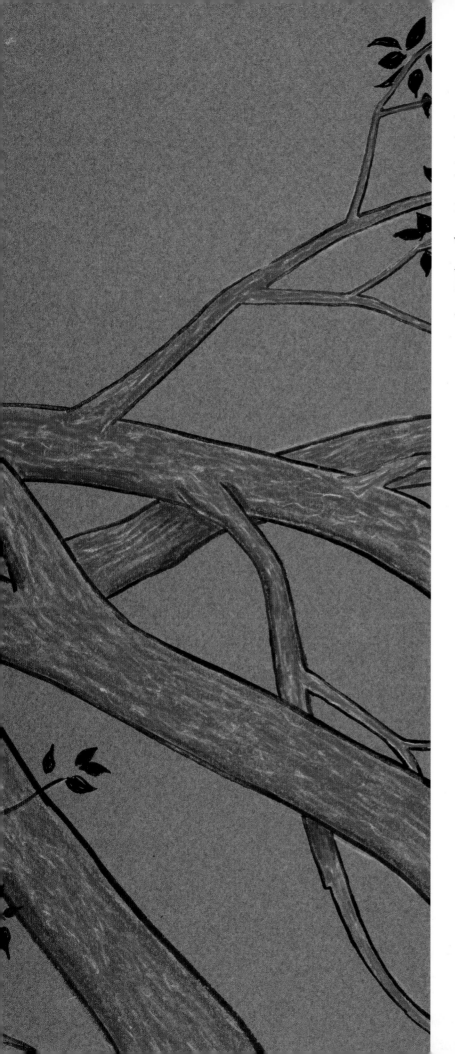

Confused and heartbroken, Rabbit could not muster the strength to go any further. He wiggled his way under a pile of dogwood branches and closed his tear-filled eyes.

He was awakened by a great white light. He rubbed his eyes and stretched his neck, trying to see through the light.

He heard a voice. "Do not be afraid, Rabbit. I know that you are looking for Jesus. He is not here, for He has been raised from the tomb."

"I am not afraid," answered Rabbit, "but I wanted to find Him. I have brought Him a gift."

"Rabbit, you have already given the one gift that Jesus treasures more than any other. You have opened your heart to receive His love. Therefore, He is with you always.

"Now take your eggs and share them with children everywhere, to remind them of the gift of eternal life that God has given to all the Earth."

Rabbit picked up the basket and rushed away from the empty tomb.

He hopped from home to home, leaving a beautiful egg for each child. He gave all he had except one – the egg he had cracked. When Rabbit returned home and placed the egg on his mantel, he saw the cross in the egg and remembered his special time with Jesus.

The Beginning.